P9-DWD-906

Being Me

written by Rosemary McCarney
illustrated by Yvonne Cathcart

Second Story Press

Rosie was up in her thinking tree,
wondering about something.
What should I be when I grow up?

Rosie didn't know the answer, but she knew she didn't like the question. It sounded like she could only *be* something when she was grown-up. That made Rosie feel unimportant… not very useful…a little smaller…as if she would only matter when she got big.

"How should I know what I want to be?" she asked herself. "I'm still a kid!"

Rosie knew she was too young to be a pilot...

or a paramedic...

or a dog groomer…

or a peanut farmer, but she could still *do* lots of terrific things.

She just needed to figure out what they were. There was plenty of time for that.

Rosie's dad came outside. He could hear her talking to herself, but he couldn't see her. "Rosie? Where are you?" he called.

"Up here, Dad!" She flapped her red cape so he could spot her.

"Everything okay?" he asked. "Anything I can help with?"

Rosie explained her problem. Her dad thought for a moment. "Let's take a walk," he said. "Maybe something will come to us."

Rosie didn't need to think about that. She was down the tree and beside her dad in a flash – a red flash.

They skipped and hopped and ran and talked for about fifteen minutes. Then they stopped in front of an old, tired-looking building. Rosie had never been here before. The sign out front read, WELCOME TO THE FOOD BANK.

"It says we're welcome, Dad," Rosie said.

"Well, what are we waiting for? Let's go in and see what this is all about."

Rosie took her father's hand as they walked up to the door.

WELCOME TO
THE FOOD BANK

Inside there was a huge warehouse filled with activity. Lots of people – very young and very old – were packing cartons with cans and packages of food. Hundreds and hundreds of boxes were piled high. A man came to greet them.

"I'm Mr. Santino, the manager," he said. "Would you like to see what we do here?"

Without thinking, Rosie yelled, "YES!"

Both men laughed. Rosie could already tell that something special was happening in this place.

Mr. Santino showed them around and explained how the food cartons were packed.

"Could I try?" Rosie wanted to know. She looked at her dad.

He nodded his head. "I'd like to try too, if that's all right with you, Mr. Santino."

Mr. Santino didn't answer, but he smiled and handed them each a carton. Because it was their first time, he stayed until they got the hang of it. At first they were quiet as they counted cans and checked items off their lists.

Before long, Mr. Santino began to talk.

"When I was your age, both of my parents lost their jobs. If we didn't have enough to eat, we would come to a place just like this for help. I will always remember the wonderful woman who ran that food bank. She was so kind. I knew that I wanted to help people too. I wasn't much older than you when I started volunteering."

Rosie felt important…useful…a little bigger…like she really mattered. *I knew I could do something before I grew up,* she thought.

When they were finished packing, Rosie and her dad helped load the food boxes onto a truck.

"Where is all this food going, Dad?" Rosie asked. "To children in other countries?"

"No, honey. There are hungry people all over the world – even here in our own town. These boxes are going to them."

Rosie tilted her head…and…

CRASH!! She forgot what she was doing, and her carton hit the ground.

Rosie bent to pick up the spilled cans and spotted a worn pair of sneakers. They were just like her friend Sam's. In fact, they were Sam's!

Rosie stood up to say hello, but Sam turned away and hurried over to his mother. To Rosie's surprise, Mr. Santino was giving Sam's mom a box of food!

For the rest of the day, Rosie worried about Sam. She hoped he wasn't embarrassed because his family needed food from the food bank, but she was pretty sure he was. How could she make him feel better? What could she do?

Tilt your head, Rosie the Red, she told herself. And she did. She tilted it this way and that…that way and this…and finally…it worked!

By bedtime, Rosie had a plan.

At school the next day, Rosie waited until everyone was drawing pictures during art. Fadimata and Sam were at her table, but Sam hadn't looked at Rosie all day. She took a deep breath.

"What would you think about having a canned food drive at school for the food bank? Everyone could help! Fadi, you could mention it in the morning announcements...and Sam..."

Sam stopped drawing but didn't look up.

"...you're an amazing artist! You could make a poster. I can't draw worth beans."

She held up her picture to prove it. A little laugh sputtered out of Sam before he could stop it. He looked up to see Rosie and Fadimata grinning at him.

Sam flipped his paper over and sketched an idea.

"Sam, it's perfect!" Rosie squealed.

Fadi agreed. "But what should the poster say?"

At the top Sam wrote: Give to the Food Drive.

At the bottom Rosie wrote: *Do* What You *Can*.

Rosie's cape flap-flapped as she
rushed home. Now she could
answer the question "What do you
want to be when you grow up?"
She would tilt her head and say,
"I'm Rosie the Red. I'm happy to *be* me.
There's no telling what I'll *do* next!"

Library and Archives Canada Cataloguing in Publication

McCarney, Rosemary A., author
Being me / written by Rosemary McCarney ;
illustrated by Yvonne Cathcart.

(A Rosie the red book)
ISBN 978-1-927583-93-7 (hardback)

I. Cathcart, Yvonne, illustrator II. Title. III. Series: McCarney, Rosemary A. Rosie the red.

PS8625.C374B45 2016   jC813'.6   C2015-908366-4

Text copyright © 2016 Rosemary McCarney
Illustrations copyright © 2016 Yvonne Cathcart
Design by Melissa Kaita

Printed and bound in China

Second Story Press gratefully acknowledges the support of the Ontario Arts Council and the Canada Council for the Arts for our publishing program. We acknowledge the financial support of the Government of Canada through the Canada Book Fund.

Published by
Second Story Press
20 Maud Street, Suite 401
Toronto, Ontario, Canada
M5V 2M5
www.secondstorypress.ca